With Best
Daw

E.Q

ANOTHER STEP INTO MY WORLD

Edwin David Bowen

Published by
Quoin Publishing Ltd.
17 North Street
Middlesbrough
TS2 1JP

About the Author

The author spent the first 25 years of his life in Gainford, where he attended the village school and his final year at Barnard Castle S.M.

As a youngster he helped on local farms and was a keen breeder and exhibitor of Dutch and English rabbits.

On leaving school he did two years' practical farm work with day-release classes before becoming a resident student at Durham School of Agriculture Houghall and has worked in farming ever since.

Over the years he has kept and shown all manor of cage birds, bantams, goats, dogs, Welsh ponies and cobs. Until recently he was an active member of the South Durham & North Yorkshire Driving Club and was seen on the road every day with various ponies.

His interest in wildlife started him writing in the early 1950s. He has two sons and two step-sons and now lives in Darlington with his wife June and collie dog, Jess.

His numerous hobbies include country and western and folk music, for which he has written songs for both genres.

In dedication to my late mother, who used to say:
"Therre is no such word as 'can't',
Find a way or make one."

Acknowledgements

I, the sole author and illustrator of this book of verse, wish to thank my typist Kathryn Hird and my wife, June, for all her help and patience and endless cups of tea. Thanks also to the people who mostly unknowingly have given me inspiration.
Happy reading.
E.D.B.

Other titles by the author:
Travellers' Joy
For All Seasons
Step Into My World
Still available with profits to G.N.A.A.

Cover picture: The author with his beloved Gemma.

Contents

Spring

The Urge

As usual it was night
And really quite late
When I felt the urge to write
But I managed a verse or two to create
And when I'd got to that stage
I don't know how it came to me
The rest just spewed out on to the page
Without the slightest difficulty.
I wrote until my eyes were sore and wrist was aching
And in my haste the curtains I hadn't drawn
And before I knew first light was breaking
So as I scribbled I witnessed the dawn
That is how it is for me
When my mind is locked on poetry.

The Parliament

From their vantage point up high
In naked branches that reach for the sky
The vigilant rooks can see, all of their territory
They know what's coming rain or snow, friend or foe
Far sooner than those down below.

As Two Became One

As I trod the familiar bare earth path
Worn smooth by generations of feet long past
Along the way I saw snowdrops and celandines
Jewels, in early spring's crown cast
In the distance I could hear the roaring Greta
Then she came into view between the trees
I stood there marvelling at her beauty
Saw her later join the in spate Tees
Then as one they went together
Tempestuously down the vale
It was then I understood why poets and authors
Years ago, to Teesdale came
To capture in words, or paint this vision
Of woods and water, whichever the season might be
Of two mighty rivers coming together
In their race towards the sea.

A Spring Dawn

I set out in the very early morning
Or would one say; the latter part of night
For in the sky not yet a hint of light
Though soon a new day would be dawning.
Within the hour, small birds to each other were calling
For the pale moon had faded out of sight,
Replaced by golden streamers watery bright.
Revealing a crystal sharp, winters spring morning
Although the grass was crunchy with white frost
And a cool breeze made the snowdrop bells flutter
To me, it seemed, winter, the battle had lost
For in hedge bottoms I found celandines, the colour of butter
And on hidden banks, gold nuggets randomly tossed
Primroses, in an array of splendorous clutter.

She Said

Black is black
And white is white
Whichever I choose
I'm always right.

Ode to a Mouse

A skin so supple and coat so shiny
Big dark blue eyes for one so tiny
Whiskers that twitch, ears that catch every sound
Telling you if there's danger around
Tiny velvety feet, prehensile tail
Only in one department do you fail,
And with this fault you have to be content
You couldn't help being created, incontinent.

The Kestrel

From his vantage point up high
He sees all below that passes by
Riding the currents of hot air
For as long as he likes he can stay up there
Till his thermal heated imogen vision
Causes him to stoop on a deadly mission
Then one poor unsuspecting vole
Has failed to make it to his bankside hole.

Magical and Mysterious

Her body's lean, her coat tawny
Her black tipped ears and brown eyes alert
She can hop leisurely about her business
Or if needs be put on a spurt.

She can lie almost flat in the pasture
Where the grass is nobut very tall
Barely visible. or detectable, when seated
For she gives off very little scent at all.

She can outrun any fox or lurcher
And knows well her own territory
But, to the poachers lamp
I'm afraid is easy quarry.

In winter the sparsest of herbage
Will fill her daily need
But, come March she boxes and prances
With others, in her urge to breed.

After which we see her less each day
Till her young have been born
Safely hidden from danger
In some secret form.

After a few hours when they're strong enough
She deposits each in turn elsewhere
And instils in them by instinct
To stay round about, just there.

She visits each location morning and evening
To suffice their daily need
And spends her time in between resting
And finding tasty things on which to feed.

And if the spring's been warm and fine
To her the weather being kind
Come May, June, she'll be frolicking in the pasture
With others of the same mind.

And so a second litter may be reared
Before the combine comes along
And the safe haven of corn stalks
Are cut and forever gone.

Then as autumn days grow shorter
And the stubbles are ploughed and bare
At the sheep troughs and the hayracks
We sometimes see our hare.

Or by the kale field or the turnips
When snow lay on the ground
We see her signature foot prints
Telling us she's been around.

And on such bright chilly winter mornings
When there's only a robin to sing
We may see our magical mysterious hare
And hope she survives till spring.

On An April Morning

As I watch through the bedroom window pane
The cows docile meander up the lane
And see in the early morning light
The lark up from the meadow take flight
To that blue sunlit place
And sing it's said, at Heavens gate
While blackbird in the bush below
Disturbs hawthorn blossom to fall like snow
I see down the avenue the chestnut trees
White candelabras swaying in the breeze
And yellow trinket flowers on the laburnum bush
While the olive speckled thrush
From topmost bough of crab apple tree
Treats all around to his repetitive melody
And dewdrops hang from leaves and blades of grass
Like multi coloured beads of glass
And amongst all this I feel insignificant and small
But oh so pleased to be alive and part of it all.

Rising Sap

When the breeze blows warm upon my face
I think of little else but you
For I am caught up in loves race.

When emotions move at frantic pace
What am I supposed to do
When the breeze blows warm upon my face?

When my thoughts are neither in order or place
And everything in life seems askew
For I am caught up in loves race.

When spring comes round innocent and chaste
All in life, young, fresh and new
When the breeze blows warm upon my face.

I cannot sleep, food has little taste
My being's as frail as morning dew
For I am caught up in loves race.

I cannot fight or give up the chase
For I have found a heaven it's true
When the breeze blows warm upon my face
For I am caught up in loves race.

Summer

The Pilgrimage

About this time, the beginning of May
I start to get itchy feet
For I know that soon
Come the month of June
Old friends on Appleby I'll meet.

For it's always around this time of year
People take to the open road
With horses and carts, and living vans
Kids, dogs, pots and pans
They become folk of the abode.

For mile upon mile they plod the drom
With their chattels and mobile homes
It's happened ever since time begun
Through wind and rain and hot June sun
Something urges them to roam.

On the flat they ride at banks they walk
As the horses heave and strain
With weight in the collar tight is the trace
Or where breeching and brake dictate the pace
And the driver's skill on the rein.

They yoke early in the morning
And drive till the sun is high
Then it's daytime camp in some shady lane
And off when the sun goes down again
Till dusk creeps into the sky.

They come from the north, the south and the east
They come from the land to the west
With horses and carts and accommodations
Joyous reunions with friends and relations
On the way to the fair they love best.

And when they reach old Appleby town
They'll stay for a week or so
And wheel and deal and buy and sell
Drink and sing, and maybe fight as well
Till back on the road it's time to go.

In the Right Place at the Right Time

On a Sunny morn in early June
I heard, both Blackbird and Thrush
From their selected boughs
Burst forth in melody,
While Sparrows and Linnets flirted
In each wayside bush,
A Lark, that pilgrim of heaven and earth
From a clear sky, poured his sweet minstrelsy,
Noisy Rooks were busy in nearby trees,
A charm of Goldfinches passed in a rush
A Curlew his shrill notes cried,
As he rose, majestically,
Swallows swooped, and Lapwings soared
It was a time, not to be ignored.

The Lengthman

With his left leg forward, back slightly bent
His strong arms swing the scythe steadily
Each cut of grass falling where it is meant
Into straight swaths readily
Then after a while, when he feels the need
He upends the sned, his arm along the blade
Using his stone with skill and speed
Till a razor sharp edge again is made
Then off he goes mowing his way
Repeating this till the close of day
And the grass verge is left shorn
As close as any manicured lawn.

Summer Songster

The lark he rose up from the meadow
In the early morning light
At heavens gate he fluttered
To those below quite out of sight
Yet all on that tapestried farmland
Heard from somewhere in the blue
Every sweet note he uttered
As he hung betwixt the two
Through morning afternoon and evening
He poured forth his melody
Before lamps were lit and windows shuttered
He plummeted back to the meadow green
With his mate to spend the night
Till the first rays of morning light.

The Path

Beneath the trees a dappled path
Lies invitingly before me
On one side a steep ivy clad bank
On the other the Tees in summer glory.

Around protruding boulders her shallow brown waters
With white ripples wend their way
Her surface in places shaded by trees
In others, caught in the suns bright rays.

In places where the waters deep
The silver grayling jump for the unwary fly
In still depths shaded by the trees
The lazy brown trout lie.

Fed by the Balder, the Greta and numerous streams
From fells and moors higher up the dale
Towards the sulphur spa at Gainford
She tumbles down the vale.

For over sixty years with various dogs
I've trod the path to the spa from the sixty-seven
In all seasons rain, sow, wind and shine
Tis here, I'm at home and in my heaven.

Conversation in a Cornfield

The barley said to the wild oat
"What are you doing in my field?
You grow so tall and unsightly
And you will contaminate my yield."

The wild oat said to the barley
"Although you were planted, and I'm here by chance
Have I not the same right as you?
In the breeze to sway and dance."

The barley said, "You have no value
You're not a proper grain
I was scientifically bred
I'm of a certain strain."

The wild oat replied, "I'm a survivor
And for your pedigree don't give two hoots"
Then the farmer came along
And pulled him up by the roots.

Then the barley whispered on the breeze
"I have no wish to gloat
But I was fairly certain that would happen
To that troublesome wild oat."

I Remember

I remember when I was a child
The golden corm fields on their headlands
Had red poppies growing wild.

And how the lark would shoot up to the sky,
And sing, a dot before the sun
As the horse drawn binder clattered by.

And how the rabbits and brown hares would run
And jink, across the stubble bare
To outwit the farmer with his gun.

And men in collarless tick shirts and trousers navy blue
Would gather up the sheaves to stand in stooks
To let the wind blow through.

And those same men again would come,
Days later, when the grain was ripe and straw was dry
And with long forks, load carts, and bring the harvest home.

To where other brown armed men with strong backs
Would toil and use their skill to forge
The great mass of sheaves into shapely stacks.

Which would b e thatched to turn the snow and rain
And at dusk, would look like galleons sailing against an autumn sky
Until months later when the thresher men came.

Then grain and straw went their separate ways.
And sweat was lost again, and thirsts were sated
On those noisy, dusty, often bitter cold days.

Ode to August

I notice that the mornings and evenings are a little sharper
Though still bright and sunny is each day
And dusk now falls a little sooner
So the blackbird flutes his days farewell a little earlier
As the year gently starts to slip away
I notice the flowers from the briar are falling
And knots of green brambles have started to form
The pink and white dog rose is no more
Her petals gone with the morning breeze
Leaving orange hips upon the thorn
I notice wild geese are on the move again
Gleaning fields where corn once waved like a golden sea
For these are harvested now and only meagre pickings remain
Straw dry in the shed, grain safe in the granary.

Memories of Field House

At Field House four shorthorn cows were kept
Two red with a minimum of white and two roan
They weren't the chunky beef type
Neither were they NDSs all skin and bone.

In my school holidays at the farm
My days were usually planned
And very often I used to milk
The two red ones by hand.

From a three legged stool two at the front
One at the back so it couldn't tip
Ankles crossed, bucket between your knees
So it couldn't slip.

Shoulder tucked into a great warm side
Your cheek against hair as smooth as silk
The rhythmic drumming on the pail
Froth rising on the top of the milk.

The sound of her stomach rumbling
The smell of meadow hay
Who could ask for a better job
To either start or end your day.

N.D.S. = Northern Dairy Short Horn.

Have You Ever

Have you ever taken your ease
And walked in summer beside the Tees
And watched swifts swoop to feed on guided wing
While from each bough the songbirds sing.

Have you ever seen the rabbits scurrying about
Heard the noisy rooks caw and shout
Or watched the silver grayling rise
Out of the water catching flies.

Have you ever laid flat beneath the willows
Reaching gently into the shallows
And tickled the lazy trout
Trying to land the slippery blighters out.

Have you ever seen a fox come to the brink
Nervously look about then take a drink
Or watched a big brown hare
Having spotted you, sit up and sniff the air.

Have you ever seen the iridescent damsel flies
Like mini helicopters fall and rise
Or a family of stoats at play
Or a heron take up and leisurely flap away.

Have you ever found and thrown
A blue sausage shaped stone
High in the air and watched it spinning drop
And heard it break the waters surface with a plop.

Have you ever taken a flat stone in your fist
And thrown it low with a flick of the wrist
Then counted the skips it makes
A game known as ducks and drakes.

These are pleasures for which you don't need to be clever
So, have you ever?

The Olde Farmer's Tale

I was sitting in the sunshine
Taking my midday ease
Enjoying a flask of tea
And sandwiches of ham and cheese.

When I spied a movement in the grass
Near the granary steps
So I stayed stock still and witnessed
Two rats doing something I'll never forget.

As first I thought they were playing
Then I realised they had a task
I had to remain patient and silent
For I couldn't go over and ask.

The object they were struggling with
Turned out to be an egg
And having manoeuvred it to the foot of an incline
One rat sat up, as if to beg.

While the other tipped and held the egg on its end
The beggar then wrapped all four legs around
Held tight, rolled on his back, then his mate
Pulled him by his tail along the ground.

Having reached where they wanted to be
They stopped for what seemed like a consultation
Squeaking and chattering and looking up the steps
So I assumed the top was their destination.

Then as if they'd come to an agreement
Both sat up face to face
Wriggled and shuffled the egg on end between them
Till they had it safely in place.

I couldn't believe what I was seeing
I just sat sandwich poised in mid air
Then by some unseen signal together they leapt
And rats and egg landed safe on the bottom stair.

Six times they repeated this process
And were half way up to the top
When the farm cat appeared and they scarpered
Letting the precious egg drop.

I really felt a twinge of sympathy
But the pair weren't to be outdone
They reappeared and dined in situ
After the cat had gone.

Now I can't say whether this story is true
Or if it's just fantasy
But I have relayed it more or less
Just as the old farmer told it to me.

Folklore of the Tees

It is said in folklore of the Tees
When there's heavy rain and the river floods
That Peg Powler a malevolent river hag
Washes her hair and the white froth is the suds.

It is said when the river is calm
That she lurks down in the deep
Coming up to drag naughty paddling children
Down to a watery permanent sleep.

It is said that sometime centuries ago
This old hag, by villagers was seen
She had sharp features, long teeth, bony hands
And was coloured all over green.

The story says she was midstream of the river
Sitting on some large protruding rocks
Soaping and busily rinsing
Her waist length straggly locks.

Now at certain times of the year
On the water an abundance of froth is there
And we believe that somewhere in Teesdale
Peg Powler is washing her hair.

The Tale of the Ghost of White Emma 1993

If you take the lane at the west end of the village
That leads to the cemetery beyond the school
Then take the narrow path
Past Gainford Wath
Around the corner lies Boat Pool.

Go upstream from her dark brooding waters
Carry on through the bower of trees
To the grassy place
Where another wath's waters race
And Barforth Hall lies just over the Tees.

To the left of the hall on the hillside
Stands a dovecot, and a chapel in ruins
From where the ghost of White Emma
Made village folk tremor
With its mysterious comings and goings.

Fishermen in the dusk of the evening
And courting couples out late at night
Told of a banshee like wailing
As down the hillside came sailing
Wreathed in mist, an object all white.

Word spread round the village like wildfire
And no doubt the locals were scared
But one man, more brave than the rest,
Said he'd do his best
To find out what it was if he dared.

So one night he set out for the river
Along with a stout stick and his dog
The breeze signed through the trees
And the moon shone on the Tees
As he settled down to wait on a fallen tree log.

He hadn't been there half an hour
When wailing broke the silence of the night
He felt cold, he felt hot
But was rooted to the spot
When into view came the object of white.

Slowly it came down the hillside
Bealing and panting all the way to the brink
The dog didn't bother and the man realised
That there before his eyes
Was a white shorthorn bull stirk, taking a drink.

Now old Walter Elland told me this story
And that leaves us in somewhat of a fix
Was it after his birth in 1892
Or is it just legend or simply not true?
I think the secret died with him in 1966.

Small but Deadly

Today I watched a spider crawl
Steadily up the kitchen wall
From skirting board to ceiling
And not for a minute had I the feeling
That it was going to fall.

And when it reached its destination
It crept into a webbed crevice without hesitation
Then just sat motionless there
Till some fly of its net quite unaware
Became the object for assassination.

Then with great speed
Spurred on by hunger and greed
Dashed out and paralysed the tangled fly
That had no option but to die
As the spider began to feed.

The Hammer and the Anvil

One evening whilst out walking
Along a bridleway
I heard a thrushes grand finale
To the dying day.

Then the song, stopped short without warning
And he flew down from his perch in the tree
And alighted, again on ivy clad wall
Not far away from me.

He searched about till he found a snail
With it clasped in his bill looked around
Till he spied a large stone
Lying not far away on the ground.

There he hammered five minutes or more
Till he cracked his prey's mobile home
Picked out the juicy morsel
Threw back his head and it was gone.

Then back he flew to the very same bough
High in that gnarled oak tree
And once more was lost
In repetitive rapturous melody.

This Time

In the moonlight the timid little vole
In search of food leaves his bank side hole
And in a split second
A force with which cannot be reckoned
Swoops from the sky
And he is destined to die
But quick as a flash
He makes a dash
And some how reaches safety
And this time, the owl goes hungry.

Autumn

Short Shift the Swift

In dizzy flight they fly non-stop
Black sickle shapes in the evening skies
Round the Old Hall's chimney pots
Feeding on the warm weather's flies
Usually last to arrive and first to be gone
Very soon this screeching hoard
Their vacation here not very long
Will be heading for warmer climes abroad
But sure as spring; after winter will follow
They, one day, will be back again
After Sand, House Martin; and Swallows
Have returned to their own domain
And we'll stand again on warm summer nights
And marvel at their dynamic flights.

The True Difference

Please tell me, because I wish to know
Whether you are a rook or a crow
You see so many times I've heard it said
And I think once in some book read
As a guide, a crow in a crowd is a rook
And a rook by himself is a crow.

So quite candidly I put it to you
Do you believe this maxim to be true
Or is it some old wives tale
Flawed, and guaranteed to fail
For some days I see you all alone
Other times of your kind there's quite a few.

Well you may see a few crows together
Depending on food availability and the weather
But we rooks are very gregarious
We like company, so there's usually a lot of us
But I suppose odd times you may see a rook on his own
Though I'm seldom alone if ever.

But if it's a true and sure way you seek
Numbers, colour or the way we speak
Won't tell you if it's my cousin or me
That you have happened to see
The real identifying secret is
I have no feathers round my beak.

Rose

I've a deerhound, greyhound, collie cross
That goes by the name of Rose
She can jump like a stag, has a head full of brains
And Lord you should see how she goes.

Now I'm not the sort of bloke to brag
But she seems ideal to me
The other night we were out on the hares
And she killed three out of three.

On a winters night when after pheasants
She just stands at the foot of each tree
As with a pole I topple them from their roosts
She dispatches them silently.

She's steady with ferrets yet quick as a flash
Has never been known to whimper or bark
And if somebody's about doesn't need to be told
Like a shadow she melts into the dark.

But she must always have an eye on me
'Cos of losing her I have no fear
For when the danger's past, wherever I am
At my side she will appear.

After the Shower

The raindrops hung from the top rail
All in a pearly row
Then one by one they steadily dropped
On to the rail below
Seconds later from number two to three
I watched as if spellbound
As to the fourth they fall rhythmically
Then with a musical sound
Plopped into waiting puddles
On the sodden ground.

A Stately Remnant

Gone with the summer days
Are the willow herbs fuchsia towers
Now in October cotton wool streamers
Replace her flowers
Yet with her now matt crimson leaves
She's still a sight to be seen
As she overlooks the tawny herbage
That in July was green.

Against a backdrop of hawthorn hedge
Whose dark branches show through leaves now yellow
Crowned in pearly dew caught in the morning sun
She depicts the majesty of a season mellow.

October Mornings at Ketton

When out walking by the river, in the early morning hour
When each hedge and tree are decked in crystal beads,
And there's pheasants, and there's partridge, a feeding on the stubble
Then a water hen runs for the sanctuary of the reeds.

Across the river sheep are grazing, blue marks upon their backs
Showing that the raddled tup has had his way
And in the distance I see Reynard, heading for his home
Where he will safely sleep the daylight hours away.

While a blackbird in the scant clad thorn, still flutes a note or two
And a robin sings hoping a mate to please
There's still places where the weakly morning sun has not yet
reached
Where frosted stalks of dead grass tremble in the breeze.

Then the donkey that stood quiet, and patient, by the paddock gate
Suddenly lets out one almighty hideous bray
For his enormous ears have heard the tractor up the lane
And now he knows his breakfast's on its way.

At the noise a flock of resting plovers suddenly take flight
Then settle with ballerina ease
But the startled roe buck that was browsing on the wheat
Heads off at speed for a nearby clump of trees.

And as I walk this bridle path beside the meandering Skerne
I'm grateful for everything I see
Who needs the expense, and hassle of foreign holidays
When there's magic, like this, at home and its all free.

It All Happens in Darlington

Our streets are patrolled on dark nights
By gangs of hooded youths on bikes with no lights
They just seem to ride around aimlessly
Causing havoc and viewing folk suspiciously.

Then speeding off into the dark
To congregate noisily in the park
In the mornings the evidence is plain to see
Beer cans and condoms from their debauchery.

Mid morning brings out the unmarried mothers
Three abreast across the pavement with no concern for others
Each armed with cigarettes and pushchair
Bare midrifted they march without a care
Most have a mobile phone clagged to their ear
And are holding loud conversations for all to hear.

Yet on they march with military precision
Be mown down or jump it's your decision
Catching your breath you turn to the rear view
And see above the hipsters and thongs most sport a tattoo.

To stay put and complain would have been of no use
All you would have got is sore shins and verbal abuse
The papers tell us of murders, assaults and drugs
What are we to do with this generation of thugs?

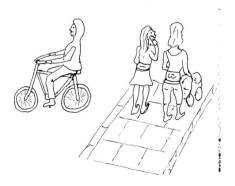

Brown and Green Seas

The ploughman ploughs his lonely way
Steadily up and down
Changing stubbles of fawn and green
Into shiny brown.

The muck has long since been spread
And he'll plough till his watch says five
The trees give the appearance of being dead
But in the spring they'll all come alive.

Gulls wheel about behind the plough
And the rooks cautiously follow
As darkness comes they disappear
But they'll all be back tomorrow.

Swaledale

O'er hill and glen
Roam dogs and men
Oft'times with little sleep
Their bred in calling in life
After a cosy home and happy wife
Is to tend to their beloved sheep
Through rain and snow
These brave men go
O'er sunny lands untamed and free
Where the red grouse and curlew cry
And purple heather rolls up to the sky
For as far as they eye can see
A rugged, harsh and beautiful place
Home to the horned sheep with the frosted black face.

Seasons New

Now gone is summers gentle breeze
An autumn winds blow hard and strong
And rips the dying leaves from trees
Now daylight's short and darkness long.

The stubble fields have been ploughed up
Worked and sown with winter corn
Amongst the ewes the randy tup
Isn't daunted or forlorn.

The squirrels made his winter store
The hedgehogs found somewhere warm and dry
The swallows have left for some distant shore
While rooks are tossed in a dismal sky.

The rowan, holly and hawthorn bushes
Are cledded red for the hungry hoards
Of redwing, fieldfares and migrant thrushes
Who will visit us from abroad.

Then October's gone and November here
And days turn frosty, dry and cold
The bright eyed robin sings our hearts to cheer
As winter's days start to unfold.

A Gifted Woman

Brown eyed, dark haired was the gypsy girl
Who came knocking at my door
Her tanned completion framed in a head square
Her garb, a shawl, long dress and pinafore.

"Would you like to buy some white heather
Hazel pegs or a lucky charm?"
As her gold banded fingers offered her wares
From the basket slung on her arm.

She said "I'm the seventh daughter of a seventh daughter
For silver I'll read your hand
You've a kindly face, and I have the power
To tell how you're future is planned".

I handed over two half-crowns
She took my hand and went into a trance
As her finger traced the lines of my palm
she began her spiel, about journeys and romance.

Of how I would have to cross water
Although they'd only be streams
Into a village not far away
To marry a girl I'd known since my teens.

I didn't really believe her story
Till she told me things from my past
Things that had happened long long ago
After that her spell was cast.

She said "I may be this way, next springtime
May I call and see how you're getting on?"
Then with a nod, and a wave of her hand
Into the autumn night she was gone.

Funnily I've never seen her since that day
But the things she told me have all come true
And everything that's happened's been beyond my control
So she must have been one of the chosen few.

I look and Listen, He Watches and Sings

As I walk this woodland path
Beside the dark ever moving Tees
I hear a robin sing his reedy song
From amongst the green lemon leafed trees.

And as I carry on my way
The song follows me as he moves from bough to bough
But when I stop, he falls silent
As if he knows I'm looking for him now.

Then when I set off again, he sings
Non-stop, not intermittently
And when again I stand, he stops
Wishing to remain anonymous while watching me.

Every night we play this game
As my dog and I walk up from the spa
This wild yet friendly woodland chorister
Screnades me, back to my car.

His Majesty

I saw him, front feet on a hillock
His coat a rusty red
A pair of antlers like oak branches
Adorned his magnificent head.

Luckily I was down wind of him
So he got no scent of me
And I could watch him as long as he stayed
From where I happened to be.

He was at least quarter of a mile away
From my well camouflaged den
But my powerful binoculars brought him within touching distance
This monarch of the glen.

The Party in the Orchard

Beware for it's now October
The main month of summer and winter between
The time of curses, spells and magic
In preparation for Halloween.

When gone is summer's glory
And trees stand stark 'neath a sky of grey
Longer are the hours of darkness
Cold are the hours of day.

When frost patterns the window panes
And fallen leaves lie crisp and white
And a cold breeze carries the eerie voices
Of witches far into the night.

As they chant the words of their magic
From the moon a cloud drifts away
Revealing shadowy figures in the woodland glade
All caught in her silvery rays.

Round a pot on a fire three are gathered
Stirring and chanting as though in a trance
While in a circle ten or twelve others
Performed some crazy dance.

Then the church clock put its hands up to its face
And chimes twelve times from its lofty tower
As bats from the belfry head for the wood
For now is the witching hour.

Then each of the coven dipped a cup in the pot
To get some of the evil brew
And on their broomsticks rode into the night
To curse in verse, people like me and you.

Then suddenly all became deathly quiet
Not a sound or a soul in sight
Except for our black cat stalking about
Her green eyes as chill as the breeze of the night.

I thought I'd been dreaming next morning
Till I found the mark where the fire had been
Twas then I remembered the village kids had dressed up
For last night was Halloween.

All From Nature's Larder

Sloes for making gin liqueur
Elder berries for wine
Brambles for pies and jam
Hazel nuts for Christmas time
Fish from the nearby river
Hares and rabbits off the land
Pheasants, partridge woodpigeon
Wild duck off the farmer's pond
If where they are I happen to stray
Soon into our kitchen they find their way.

Third Hand

A stoat had just killed a rabbit
And to cover was dragging it away
When from the sky stooped
A bird of prey.

But unfortunately for both
A fox was passing by
So the stoat scarpered
And the hawk again took to the sky.

The fox without any effort
Had secured himself his lunch
And after his meal retired to sleep
Feeling as proud as punch.

Till he heard that dreaded sound the horn
Far off in the distance
And knew from past experience that
He should vacate the vicinity of his presence.

He wished now he hadn't gorged himself
Just wanted to rest, his meal to savour
But luckily he didn't have to hurry
As the wind was in his favour.

So he headed for the big pasture
Went straight through a flock of sheep
Then down into the river
And swam downstream where it was deep.

When he reached the other side
He trotted back upstream in the shallows
And headed for the rocky cliffs
That were all hills and hollows.

For there he had an earth
Where occasionally he would go
On reaching it he lay down at the entrance
And watched hounds a hundred feet below.

And when he awoke it was evening
The sun into the west had sank
And he again was feeling hungry
So he set off back down the rocky bank.

By the time he reached the valley
Where hounds had been that morning
The air was cool and dusk
Like a blanket was falling.

He set out on one of the many tracks
Heading east to a remote farm
Where he knew bantams often stayed out
And he might catch one without causing alarm.

Then his keen nose picked up a scent
Carried on the chill evening breeze
Next a faint yap reached his ears
Above the sound of the whispering trees.

So in an instant he decided
The owner of that voice he must find
So he off in the direction from whence it came
Food now the last thing on his mind.

He must have covered a least a mile
When he came to a clearing he knew
And there sitting in the moonlight
A beautiful vixen came into view.

He looked cautiously about
Thinking wouldn't it be great
I'll go over and introduce myself
And see if I can secure a mate.

So he checked the area twice again
And then broke his cover
Then after a brief introduction
The two new lovers left together.

The Friendly Visitor

When tidying up in the garden
Leave a few leaves in a heap
In a quiet corner, a cosy spot
Where hedgehog can get some sleep.

A place where he can curl up
Into a spiky ball
And spend the cold days almost comatose
Without being disturbed at all.

When by the first rays of spring sunshine
He's wakened from his sleep
He'll poke his head out, sniff the air
Then round the garden creep.

So if you put out a saucer of water
And a little dog meat on a tray
You'll be encouraging the eco warrior
In your garden to stay.

For he'll wage war on all the beetles
And slugs on that you can depend
For your nocturnal spiky forager
Is definitely the gardener's friend.

Old Practice of the Golden Hoof

Each morning be it fine or wet
The man comes with his collie dogs
And moves the posts and wire net
To make a fresh stint for the hoggs.

The sheep will eat each purple globe
Right down to it's root
And the green leaves into a sea of mud
Will be trampled underfoot.

When the last of the lambs have fat enough grown
And the turnips have all gone
The land will be ploughed and with barley sown
To wave golden in next summers sun.

But while the barleys green on a fine spring day
The man will fiddle it with grass and clover seed
Then after harvest will grow a three or four year ley
To be followed by a crop of wheat.

As days shorten there's not a moment to be lost
Muck spreading and ploughing must start
So the furr' can be set up for the winter frost
And the muck rot and keep the land in good heart.

Then after the sowing of all other corn
The land will be worked and tilled
In preparation for lambs that have already been born
More turnips will be drilled.

Then after hoeing, haytime and harvest are done
And you've worked as hard as you can
Out come the posts and nets in autumn sun
I know, I was that man.

Norfolk four course rotation
Roots (turnips) barley, seeds (grass) wheat

A Simple Reminder

Still each year the poppies grow.
A reminder to cach generation
For those brave souls who faced the foe.

To defend the right they were not slow
Those courageous people of our nation
Still each year the poppies grow.

They fought in desert heat and snow
Twas mud, mire and all damnation
For those brave souls who faced the foe.

They endured more than we'll ever know
A living hell of fear and starvation
Still each year the poppies grow.

And shake their pepper pots as breezes blow
Over those who were our salvation
For those brave souls who faced the foe.

Their graves stand, row after row
Their names on cenotaphs for observation
Still each year the poppies grow
For those brave souls who faced the foe.

When I'm Gone

When I am dead and gone
I wonder what people will say
Oh how he liked to hear the larks sing
On a fine spring day
And see the swallows skim the pasture
Hear the cuckoo, and smell the drying hay
Or how he liked to hear blackbird and thrush
Compete in melody from blossomed boughs
As he toiled in the fields his collie ever near
On hot summer days when sweat poured from his brow
And how he loved those winter days when cattle were inside
And the robin sang from the beam as he milked the cows
Will those who are left remember my delights
Sadly I'll never know, for I know not now.

Winter

Fluttering Flakes

We awoke to grey day weather
Snowflakes gently coming down
Each one lighter than a feather
Like a blanket o'er the town.

Snowflakes gently coming down
Covering every field and hill
Like a blanket o'er the town
So peaceful and so still.

Covering every field and hill
In a pristine layer of white
So peaceful and so still
It must have snowed all through the night.

In a pristine layer of white
Each one lighter than a feather
It must have snowed all through the night
We awoke to grey day weather.

Christmas Shopping at the Supermarket

In the car park there are fleets of cars
Waiting to come in a long procession
Though the politicians tell us
That the country's in recession.

Inside shoppers load their trolleys
As if there's no tomorrow
They're not bothered how much they spend
Even if they have to borrow.

They just keep chucking things in
As though everything is fine
Food, toys, presents, chocolates
Lager, whisky, wine.

There's folks all shapes and sizes
A real motley bunch
Spending it seems for spending's sake
They've never heard of the credit crunch.

There's some harassed looking housewives
And those without a care
Who block the isles in threes and fours
Just standing nattering there.

By now the trolley has a mind of it's own
And refuses to go straight
And all but cleans out half the queue
Who by the checkout wait.

The hold ups 'cos something's lost its barcode
And the girl has rung the bell
For another member of staff to come
How long she'll be no one can tell.

You've dashed about up and down
In the limited time you've got
You only wanted a few things
But in the end have bought a lot.

Finally your goods are on the conveyer belt
Oh, isn't that just fantastic
The chip and pin machine has jammed
And the woman in front is paying by plastic.

That problem finally solved
Your feet ache and you're feeling tired
Two articles of yours get through
Then chaos, the till roll has expired.

The poor assistant gets another out
With not so much as a grumble
And in the bowels of the till
With reams of paper has to fumble.

But every credit due to her
She manages quicker than you expected
And you and your trolley are soon on your way
Crabwise, headed for the exit.

And when you finally do emerge
Knowing where you'd like to be but not quite where you are
You stand there like an idiot
'Cos you've lost the bloody car.

A Prayer for Mankind

Oh Lord I know you're there
Please lend an ear to my prayer
It's for men and women everywhere
The people of the world.

Please Lord germinate the seed
To find the peace they so badly need
For folk of every colour and creed
The People of the world.

Let all leaders talk of peace
Cause all war mongering to cease
So they may be from their fears released
The people of the world.

So your many treasures they may see
The best of which are absolutely free
And mankind survive in love and harmony
The people of the world.

Country and Western

Wrong Time, Wrong Place, Right Woman

Well I met a girl way up in Oaklahoma
Prettiest thing a'd ever seen in all ma life
I fell in love, an like a fool a told her
Asked her if she fancied, becoming ma wife.

Now a've always been a gambler and a drifter
Never one for stayin, long in one place
Never afraid, of bein a biglifter
Always searchin, for that elusive ace.

When she smiled, a thought a'd hit the jackpot
When she winked, a felt sure a'd a winnin hand
She must have took me for a real crackpot
For bein just, too thick to understand.

She had eyes as brown as the Mississippi
Long blonde hair, piled high upon her head
A smile, like the mornin sun, when she looked at me
And blew kisses, from those lips of ruby red.

Most of the time a felt like a was dreamin
Never thought of her as a saloon hooker
And that all the while, she was a schemein
And that a was bein taken for a fool and a sucker.

A gave her money for a weddin outfit
Only too pleased, that a was her chosen one
Now the money, doesn't bother me one little bit
But ma prides been dented knowin that she's gone.

Though she did leave a note, sayin she was sorry
And that every gamblers, got to loose sometime
That she'd make out, an a was not to worry
And that she was sure, everything would work out fine

You know a never ever did forget that woman
Perhaps it was a favour, that she did for me
By takin ma cash, an up an runnin
Guess somethings in this life, ain't meant to be.

Yet in ma wallet, a still kept her picture
For deep down, a felt life could have been so good
An a hoped that in some saloon in the future
She'd be singin, Where a was sittin dealin stud.

She must have had feelins, else she wouldn't have written
A think that somehow, it was just a sad case
For a know full well, she knew a was smitten
Guess it just happened to be, wrong time wrong place.

Two years down the line,an 'am in Frankfort Kentucky
When from across the street, a hear a voice a knew so well
Up till then at the cards, a was bein lucky
But a just had to get over to that hotel.

Now there was a lot of money on the table
Over two thousand dollars in the pot
But a just folded, got up as quick as a was able
Walked away and left the bloody lot.

As a crossed that street a was fair a shakin
While strainin to catch every note the singer sang

A listened at the door prayin a wasn't mistaken
As out into the night, her clear voice rang.

When she was done, a made ma entry
Not knowin, how things would unfold
When she saw me,she ran and threw her arms around me
And a saw in her eyes, a story that needed to be told.

When she finished her spot,she came back to ma hotel room
And we sat up jawin long into the night
She told me about her years of doom and gloom
Till her husband, the brute, got killed in a gunfight.

She said, our meetin up wasn't just by chance
She'd heard about the game, and figured ad be in town
And thought that if I was still big on romance
When a heard she was singin I would track her down.

She told me how the past had been a hard teacher
And that sometimes she'd had to fight for her life
When mornin came round, we went out and found a preacher
An within three weeks, that woman was ma wife.

Very next day, we joined a wagon train for Missouri
After freedom, married life did seem a little scary
But a was hellbent she'd be happy with yours truly
On a spread of our own out on the prairie.

Thirty years on an we're still together
Although life's not always bin an easy ride
But we've come through the rough, the smooth, the stormy weather
An a'd do it all agin , with her by my side.

For it just seems we were meant for each other
Though it took a little time, to get round that way
To three girls and two fine boys she's a mother
An am the happiest proudest man, in the U.S.A.

The Reunion

He rode into the sleepy town
One sunny afternoon
Tied up at the hitchin rail
And went into the saloon.

The place went deadly quiet
As he strode up to the bar
Ordered rye whisky
And took out a thin cigar.

The Sheriff ambled over and said
"You're not from round here son
If you're plannin on stayin
Let me see your gun".

The stranger looked him in the eye
And said "If you want my weapon take it
But I advise you not to try
Unless you think that you can make it".

The Sheriff's eyes didn't flicker
But he stamped down hard on the strangers toe
As his head went down, a knee struck his chin
Then he was dealt a crashing blow.

The stranger he reached for his gun
As he lay there on the floor
But the Sheriff had cleared his leather
Before he'd had chance to draw.

He said "Now be right careful
And pass your side iron over here
Butt first, real slow like
And you'll have nothing to fear".

The Sheriff recognised the six gun
As the stranger dusted himself down
And he said "Now tell me why
You're in this back water town".

"Well I remember me Ma and Pa
When I was just a child
Then I got in with a bad lot
And started runnin wild".

"Next I heard my Pa was dyin
And how I'd lost my Mother
So I went back home to see him
And he told me a had a brother".

He said "He was a hard man
Like he'd bin in his younger days
And if I could find him
He'd help me mend ma ways".

The Sheriff said "I recognised the face
As soon as you came in
Plus the swagger, arrogance, then the gun
I knew you were my kin".

"And now you've spun your yarn
As only an O'Hennessy can
It all adds up as obvious
We both have the same old man".

"So barkeep, drinks all round
And let the music play
For you don't come across
A long lost brother every day".

Val H's Tiny Feet

When speaking to a friend of mine
Who is ever so pretty and sweet
She's not very tall
In fact, quite small
But in the bosom department
Anything but petite

She's go the loveliest of smiles
And looks that with age never fade
She always dresses so tidy and neat
From her fascinator down to her tiny feet
When I remarked on their size
She tilted her head and replied:
"Well you know Dave
Things don't grow too well in the shade"

A Load of Bull

The trail had been long and hard
The front street was dry and dusty
The sun blazed down from a sky of blue
As he rode into the town of sleepy valley.

He pulled up at the livery
And got down out of the saddle
One lean, mean looking hombre
A man with whom you shouldn't tangle

His face was weather worn and craggy
A moustache hung above his top lip
Round his narrow waist a gun belt supported
A pearl handled peace maker at each hip.

The proprietor came out, he passed the reins
Along with a two-dollar bill
Saying, "Pick his feet and rub him down
And of your best oats give him his fill."

Then he strode out across the street
To the gold nugget saloon
For first a drink and then a bath
And to see to rent a room.

His marshall's badge he kept out of sight
Not wanting to draw too much attention
As he just wanted to be all ears
And weigh up the situation

For he was on a mission
The purpose of which was this
Hearsay had it someone round about
Was growing and supplying Cannibis

So he'd been sent to this backwater
Because to the locals he wasn't known
In the hope that he could suss out
By whom and where it was being grown

But a saloon singer blew his cover
She recognised him from another town
So he came straight out and told his purpose
And that he was going to track the culprits down

In the days that followed he talked to many
And visited big ranches and small farms
Rode over acres and acres of prairie
Looked in dozens of buildings and barns

But at a shack in the foothills he was greeted
With a rifle, the old man saying, "I don't want no fuss
Just turn your horse round and clear off
Life's hard enough out here for us"

The Marshall pointed to his badge
As a means of his authority
So the old man lowered his weapon
And let him look round reluctantly

Then he gestured to a nearby hill
And said, "But don't go over there"
The Marshall again pointed to his badge
Saying, "I can go anywhere"

The old man just shrugged his shoulders
And had no more to say
As towards the hill the lawman
On foot made his way

But he came back faster than he went
Of that there was no doubt
For gaining on him rapidly
Was a bull in hot pursuit

The lawman shouted "do something
Don't just stand there like someone radge"
The farmer rolled his eyes and hollered
"Show him your bloody badge"

He Was Oh So Brave

On a fertile plateau by a river
A tribe of Indians had their home
It had woods and hills from where coyotes called
And prairie where buffalo roamed.

It was in this village in a tepee
On a morning fine and warm
That to a brave and pretty young maiden
A fine baby boy was born.

Now this was no ordinary baby
He was beautiful and oh so sweet
But after a while his mother noticed
That he wasn't quite complete.

Yes he had two arms, two legs, two feet
Two eyes, a nose, and was growing up strong
But something he should have had two of
Well this little chap only had one.

Now to these Indian people
This condition wasn't unknown
For they'd seen ponies the same
So they called this little fellow One Stone.

On becoming a man he hated the name
And made it clear his will
That anyone addressing him by this moniker
He would surely kill.

One day while walking through the village
He met Bluebird, who'd been away quite a while
So not knowing she said "Hello, One Stone"
As she greeted him with a smile.

So he lured her into the woods
And they made love hour upon hour
Till the poor maid died of exhaustion
Then he buried her in a shady bower.

A week or so later another maiden returned
Yellow Bird was her name
And her not knowing, she made the mistake
Of greeting him just the same.

Now still tired from his last encounter
But with a deep burning hatred inside
He lured her also into the wood
To avenge his injured pride.

But tougher than her cousin, she wore him down
Till his energy was all gone
So it just goes to show that you can't rely
On being able to kill two birds with one stone.

Miscellaneous

Pure Nonsense

Once upon a time there was a funny little man
And he lived on the planet zog
With his funny little wife
Two funny little children
And a very very funny little dog.

Now this funny little man was known far and wide
And he went by the name of Joe
His wife's name was Ida
And the farm where they lived
Was known as 'IdaJoe'.

Now the eldest of the children was a funny little boy
Who had a shock of curly hair the colour of fire
He had a funny little smile
'Cos his eyes weren't level
That's how he came to be called Issiah.

Now the other of the children was a pretty little girl
Who was ever so timid and quiet
She had coal black hair
And mauve blue eyes
So they'd christened her Shy Violet.

Now the funny little dog had a long shaggy coat
That really was as black as pitch
And if you didn't see it eating
Or wagging its tail
You couldn't tell which end was which.

Out on the farm they had funny ducks and geese
And hens that only laid square eggs
Funny blue cows that gave
Butter milk and cheese
And a straight tailed pig with three legs.

So now you've heard the story of the folks from planet zog
And I really think that you should go to sleep
'Cos you're tucked up nice and warm
So just close your eyes
And start counting all their pretty yellow sheep.

The Monarch and the Medic

De McIntosh said to King Edward
Your Highness may I be so bold as to say
Surrounded by Ivories and Redskins quite suits you
You look really Majestic today.

King Edward replied, "Dear cousin
You're a friend so true and so loyal
If the Records will join us shall I get Arron Pilot
To take us to visit the Jersey Royals."

I can arrange it with Maris Piper
I'm sure all will go ever so well
We can first call and see the Lincolns
And then go on to Pentland Dell.

After that fly across to Jersey
Really, just to check out their crops
Cos they think they're the creme de la creme of spuds
Being one of the first to hit the shops.

Then to round off our jaunt
Before returning home again
We'll call and see our relatives the Majorcans
On that little island off Spain.

But before this dream could happen
The right royal holiday bash
They were sold, sliced, boiled or chipped
Or served up with sausages as mash.

Crafty Old Devil

An old dales farmer got poshed up to go to market
One bright and sunny day
And he called in to see the doctor
As it happened to be on his way.

He said "Doc I've a failing
And I'd appreciate your view
But I need it kept quiet like
Just between me and you".

The Doc said "That's no problem
For I'm not at liberty
To disclose a conversation
It's called patient confidentiality".

So the old farmer he confided
The Doc did a test or two and said we can fix it
Call in a week come Monday
On your way back from the market.

So the old farmer called on the appointed day
And picked up a small device
Heard things folks thought he couldn't hear
And not all of them were nice.

Days later he happened to meet the Doc
Who asked how he was getting on
The old man said he had a different opinion
Of nearly everyone.

"Well at least your family will be pleased
That you can hear when they speak"
"Nay lad, a just sits quiet like I allus did
But a changed me will three times last week".

This Old Guy's Still Got the Patter

I've always had an Audi or Mercedes
Jaguar or Volvo
And when I was a young chap
You should have seen me make them go.

In twills, tweed jackets and yellow waistcoat
Leather driving gloves and dark glasses
Oh in those days I had all the patter
And could impress the lasses.

I've never had an accident
And have reached the age of eighty-two
But when I say this friends reply
'No, but I bet you've caused a few'.

Nowadays I never go above forty
And if there's been a shower
I drop my speed down to
A steady twenty-five miles an hour.

Drivers hoot and shake their fists at me
But I don't really care
I pay my tax and insurance
So I've as much right as them to be there.

When I want to pull over or stop
I don't bother about yellow lines
The glove compartment full of parking tickets
And letters for unpaid fines.

A policeman stopped me the other day
For what I didn't know
Guess what his excuse was
He said I was going too slow.

I said "Well I'm too old now
To go tearing about for thrills
And don't you know that on the telly, son
They keep informing us, speed kills."

As he opened his mouth to reply I said
"I know you're trying to do your best
But I was driving before you were born
And didn't need to take a test".

"I served King and Country
To make this land safer for folks like you
And because I drive with care and attention
This is what you do".

"Hassle an old man with some flimsy excuse
When he's just going quietly on his way"
And when I stopped for breath, he just shook his head and said
"Speed up granddad, and have a nice day".

Paddy on the Line

Paddy out in his car one day
Came hurtling down the centre of the street
Unfortunately for him
A policeman he'd chance to meet
The copper pulled him up saying
"You can't do that, don't you know"
Paddy says "Ah sure I can
On me licence it says so"
The policeman said "Have you got your licence?"
Paddy said, "Here it is it's fine
There's me name, Patrick Murphy
And below; tear along the dotted line."

A Time for Truth

The Priest boarded a train
To go on a journey
And found in his choice of carriage
A Rabbi for company.

Just being the two of them alone
They struck up a conversation
And found out they were both headed
For the same destination.

After much pleasant chatter
Over many miles they'd ridden
The conversation turned
To things that were forbidden.

As the train prepared to pull up
In the station at York
The Priest jokingly said "Pray tell me
Have you ever tasted pork?"

The Rabbi said "Most certainly not"
But then in a very low voice
Said "Just once after much temptation
I gave in and made the wrong choice".

"Now I've answered your question
And been sincere and true
There's a similar one to which
I'd like an answer from you".

"As a man of the Roman Catholic faith
Are you not supposed to be
Married to God and the Church
And sworn to celibacy?"

"So pray tell me the truth
And be as straight as I have with you
Have you in your term with the ladies
Had anything to do?"

The Priest hung his head
And said "To be truthful I'm afraid
Like you, may God forgive me
For the one mistake I made".

The Rabbi smiled at his honesty
And said "Bless you my son
We're only human
When all is said and done".

As the train built up steam
To pull out of the station of York
The Rabbi again turned to the Priest and said
"But sex is definitely better than pork".

Choose Your Words

When things are said that shouldn't be
In bad mood or haste
And friendships cooled or lost
Oh what a waste.

When tempers flare and harsh words
Or home truths are spoken
Life may look outwardly the same
But some inner thread is broken.

Even if rekindled
One party may always regret
The other may try to forgive
But will never forget.

So engage your brain before you speak
Think carefully about what to say
Then you just might gain respect
From those you meet along life's way.

Ode to Spike

In the Queen's birthday honours list
Do you remember? Did you happen to see?
That Spike Milligan the comedian's name appeared
As being awarded the M.B.E.

To which he replied, "We don't have an empire
So the meaning and medal are worthless to me"
A quote he sent in a printed letter
To Her Royal Majesty's secretary.

Saying also "I can learn any script and ad lib
With the Goons get laughs galore
So you might as well have bestowed on me
Life membership of the Co-Operative Store."

"And to conclude my letter a request
For which I truly ask your pardon
Would it be possible for me to paint
All the gnomes in the palace garden?"

Then just before he died he wrote
Instructions in his will
That on his gravestone it should say
I told you I was ill.

A Look Back in Time

I remember back in the 1950s
When through Gainford steam trains ran
Fred Peart was Station Master
And Arthur Bell was Signal Man.

Bill Barr ran a market garden
Which supplied Bill and Meg Scaife's fruit and veg shop
And the village boasted two butchers.
Norman Collins at the gas works end of the green
And Ray Iveson's shop at the top.

Dr. Hickey's surgery was at premises on High Row
Arthur Tennick was Miss Edleston's agent
Jack Liddle was the painter and decorator
H & J Walton the corn merchants.

Coulthards had a shop on the green
And Mrs Tailford's on the main road was most handy
Willie Coates managed the Co-Op Stores
And Mr Allen the Post Master
Had a golden spaniel called Brandy.

Jack and Ellen Millar supplied us with fish and chips
The school's headmaster was Claude Cree
George Robinson's firm made hen houses
While his brother Bob owned Gainford Hatchery.

Sam Hall was the chimney sweep
Charge Bros. stonemasons and joiners
Walter Davison ran his coal business
Jack Gillian saw to our footwear repairs
While Bob, Arthur and Albert Webb were plumbers and glaziers.

Hacketts specialised in light engineering
Old Mrs Charge taught paying pupils piano
Fawcetts supplied us with fresh farm bottled milk
And Bill Forman was caretaker of the Montalbo.

The village had three public houses
The Lord Nelson, Queen's Head and Cross Keys
The Queen's sold petrol from pumps at the front
The mine hosts in those days were,
Ronnie James, Les Naismith and George Brown respectively.

Jack Whitfield and Paddy McGuire kept the roadsides tidy
Men play snooker at the Institute, the ladies had WI
And our resident bobby P.C. Hallam
Over everything kept a watchful eye.

The Tale of Roger and Martha of Bowes

Roger Wrightson kept the Kings Head
A yeoman family born and bred
The last pub before you took on Stainmore Pass
The first you'd meet if you'd just come across.

The George was kept by John Railton
Who was a simple uncouthed man
But it was not competition that brought hate to their doors
But the fact that they might become in-laws.

For Wrightson had a fine young son
Whose handsome features glowed
And Railton had a daughter on whom
God beauty had bestowed.

What's more the two several times had met
And to them it was with deep regret
That neither set of parents thought the other
Good enough to be their offspring's lover.

And so this romance in the bud they tried to nip
But the couple started a clandestine relationship
And from that heather strewn sheep ridden land
Together to elope they planned.

But his sister Hannah told on them
And their parents intervened yet again
Forbidding them each other to see
So that their love could never be.

Roger took to wandering the moors at night
His handsome features as pale as the moon's silver light
For his spirits were low and his heart filled with dread
And in February with a fever took to his bed.

Never more his strength to regain
Broken hearted there to remain
Martha sent an orange one day
But the Wrightsons turned her gift away.

Then his parents more out of pity than love
When it seemed Roger was to be called by Him above
And there was no fear of Martha becoming his bride
Allowed her to visit his bedside.

But the spiteful Hannah by the door did stay
To hear what the couple had to say
And so with tears in her eyes
Martha softly whispered her goodbyes.

And on that dreadful cold March day
As back to the George she made her way
The death bell tolled in the village of Bowes
Telling Roger's life had come to a close.

"My heart is burst" sweet Martha said
And three hours later she too was dead
And so the bell tolled again just hours between
On March thirteenth seventeen fourteen

Afterwards neither family knew prosperity
And Hannah at Boroughbridge died in poverty
And if today you visit Bowes cemetery
There on a headstone for all to see

Buried in one grave never more to part
Though each died of a broken heart
Roger and Martha in life oppressed
In death together lie at rest.

Footnote

The King's Head was turned into a private dwelling
And of it's liquor licence shorn
The George had it's name changed
And is now the Ancient Unicorn
So if on a sunny day you pass through Bowes
Spare a thought for how things would have been
For two 20 year old lovers
In the winter of 1714.

I Think

If all the money in the world
Was given out to each member of the population
In equal shares
I'll guarantee before a two year duration
The people who have the most of it now
Would have claimed it back as theirs.

For there has to be capitalists
Who rule from their dominions
One can't have an all rich society
There must be chiefs and indians
People willing to take calculated risks
So there's work for the likes of you and me.

Three Stone Crosses on a Moorland Road

If you take the road from Castleton to Rosedale
To where the ownership lines the moor divides
You'll see a monument known as Ralphs Cross
Standing stately by the roadside.

It doesn't mark any historic event
Or bear the names of family or friends
But shows the spot where a penniless wayfarer
Through exhaustion came to life's journey's end.

He was found it is said by a farmer called Ralph
And it was he who had the cross placed there
With a hollow in the top so anyone passing
Could toss in any coins they could spare.

So any tramp or hard up traveller
Any journeyman destitute or poor
Could help himself to the price of a bite
As he crossed that bleak and lonely moor.

Three or four hundred yards to the west
Stands a cross set back hidden in the heather
It marks where two lost Catholic parties
Were reunited in the foulest of weather.

While three of four hundred yards to the east
Of Ralph's Cross, there stands for all to see
A huge roughly hewn stone pillar
Known as the White Cross or Fat Betty.

Proud like a sentinel on a neutral point
On land where the boundary lines meet
On her top a stone fashioned as a Maltese Cross
And whitewash about her feet.

So Ralph's Cross shows where a poor soul died
The half hidden one where all turned out fine
And Fat Betty in her whitewash robes
The limits to where the Guisborough monks could mine

My Super Superstitious Mam's Sayings

There are many things that stick in my mind
That my mother has done and said
Like never walk under a ladder
Always walk round instead.
For whoever is up that ladder
May let something fall on your head
But what if the ladder's across the pavement said I
Should I step out onto the road
And run the risk of being knocked down
By a car, or a wagon with a heavy load
Oh just "Watch what you're doing" she'd reply
And remember your highway code.

She always threw salt over her shoulder
If she happened to spill some on the floor
And vowed if you broke a mirror
You'd have seven years bad luck or more
She always greeted a magpie
And had a horseshoe nailed to a door
She told me when it thundered
That it was God moving his furniture about
And when it snowed she said Mother Hubbard
Was shaking her feather pillowcases out
And on the first of each month she'd say White Rabbits three times
Before she was up and about.

She would never allow new shoes on the table
And said birds brought death to your window pane
And also if you dropped a knife a stranger would call
And it wouldn't be to your financial gain
She wouldn't have any sort of blossom in the house
Or peacock feathers anywhere near
But a rabbit's foot, lucky penny or pebble charm
Were said to help drive away any fear

She always maintained opals were unlucky
Even when set in a bangle or ring
And would never entertain pearls for the same reason
Round her neck on a string.

She believed that when flowers died
Their colours went to brighten up the rainbow
And one thing she would never ever do
Was look at a new moon through a window
She kept all of her bill money
In a caddy on the high mantle shelf
And told me if I looked after the pennies
The pounds would look after themselves
I remember her counting her coppers
Out of that old caddy tin
And saying one day I'll be rich you know
When my ship comes in.

She showed me that ship on a half penny
Told me there were 480 in a £1
And said they would always keep sailing
Because coins were round and made to go round
She said if you save then spend them wisely
And not just fritter them away into the blue
One day you'll find ten fold or more
They'll all sail back to you
Funny little woman my mother
And although it's years since she passed away
In my mind I can see and hear her
Just as if it was yesterday.

The Sixties

The sixties was a decade of revolution
There was so much going on you see
Fashion wise, the pill, and a cornucopia of talent
In the music industry.

Kenny Lynch was Up On The Roof
Petula Clark was Down Town
Cilla Black was croaking Anyone Who Had a Heart
While Bobby Vee Bounced his Rubber Ball all around.

Brenda Lee was Jumpin the Broomstick
Bobby Darin had Dream Lover
The Dave Clark Five had Bits and Pieces
While Johnny Kidd and the Pirates were Shakin All Over.

The Tornadoes wowed us with Telstar
Barefoot Sandie Shaw gave us Puppet On a String
Cliff Richard was going on his Summer Holiday
While Frank Ifield was off with the Wayward Wind.

The Stones had Little Red Rooster
While the Beatles had A Hard Day's Night
The Searchers sang Sweets for my Sweet
While Lena Martel took One Day at a Time.

Aka Bilk serenaded us with Stranger on the Shore
While the Hollies gave us Hey Carrie Ann
Billy Fury was Half Way to Paradise
While Tom Jones about the Green Green Grass of Home sang.

Helen Shapiro was Walking Back to Happiness
While the Supremes had Baby Love
Hermans Hermits Two Silhouettes on the Shade
The Animals House of the Rising Sun.

Del Shannon was busy with Run Away
Buddy Hollie sang about Peggy Sue
Paul Anka was just a Lonely Boy
Dion and the Belmonts had Run Around Sue.

There were heaps of other artists
Each had good songs to sing
But the greatest of all I've kept till last
And that is 'Elvis' the King.

Those were some of the 60s songs and music
Artists whose names and work will never fade
We've had very little to compare you'll surely agree
In the last four and a half decades.

So come on folks get rockin
Give your Blue Suede Shoes a blast
There's never been another time like it
It's good to live now and then in the past.

All in the Past

All the old farmers of my youth
Have sadly passed away
But the fine cattle they bred
I will remember for many a day,.

To my young and eager mind
Those old men freely passed their knowledge
And gave me an understanding of livestock
I could never have found in a book or college.

Cecil Peacock of Hill House
In his dry and genteel manner
Taught me about his Headlam Friesians
For a weekly wage of three pounds two and a tanner.

John Harrison kept Shorthorns
And spoke at length of them with pride
He was as well known as his famous cattle
His top price bulls being sold world wide.

A beautiful herd of Ayrshires
Were kept by Major Jaffray at Snow Hall
And later black crossbred Suckler Cows
And a South Devon bull I recall.

Maurice Robson at Field House
Bred some of the finest Herefords in the north
For at the shows and Edinburgh Bull Sales
They really proved their worth.

At Park Farm Robert Harrison
An Oxford Down sheep man of fame
Sold his Shorthorns and bought Friesians
I knew every cow by name.

Now these great stocksmen of renown
Along with their herds are dead and gone
And we'll never see the like again
So now only fond memories live on.

In the Seventies

Three fifty five each Saturday afternoon
Would see me, with cup of tea
Wander through into our living room
And settle down in big armchair
Switch on TV to channel three
And for an hour be rooted there.

Brian Crabtree was usually the M.C.
And Kent Walton's commentaries were just great
Lou Marco and Max Ward were referees
Sometimes the tea was left to go stone cold
Through watching those we all loved to hate
Escaping full nelsons and strangle holds.

And though I often shouted at the screen
When disagreeing with the ref's decision
Thinking if he'd done this or that, how it might have been
But two falls two submissions or a K.O.
Needed fast thinking, guts and precision
Made better viewing than any cookery programme or game show.

For Mick McManus was the hard man with the smile
Steve Logan the king of forearm smash
Les Kellet, he mixed humour with guile
Cry Baby Brakes would scream and stamp and shout
Big Daddy would flatten 'em with his belly splash
While Cat Weasel skilfully clowned about.

The cynics used to say it was all a fix
And that all the moves where choreographed
That it wasn't strength just timely tricks
But dozens took up this athletic art
Of grown men supposedly acting daft
Yet each painfully played an entertaining part.

And if I was dragged off into town, heaven knows
I'd make sure Uptons was close around half past three
Because in those days there were no videos
And she could finish the shopping on her own again
While I with other husbands watched the shops TV's
Our noses almost touching the window pane.

Gone But Not Forgotten

John Harrison loved his Shorthorn Cattle
He knew each beast by name
And any captive audience
Was certainly fair game.

He knew each animal's pedigree
And would ramble on at length
Extolling each one's virtues
It's weaknesses it's strength.

He was a great ambassador
For the red white and roan
And through his devotion to the breed
Gainform Hall world wide is known.

The visitor's book is full of names
Of folk from both home and abroad
Who have bought from the famous families
Of Rosebud, Flora and Maud.

The Queen's Farm Manager was no stranger
To this little village near Darlington
And over the years bought white bulls
To run with the herds at Balmoral and Sandringham.

But now alas John, and his cattle are gone
To those pastures in the sky
But in some folks minds, they've left behind
Memories that will never die.

And It All Started at Ketton

Ketton Hall for centuries has been renowned
And this is still so to this day
As a farm where fine cattle can be found
Although with different breeds, it's true to say.

The brothers Robert and Charles Colling
Are names one should never ever forget
For it was in the late seventeen hundreds
They started the line that bred Comet.

They used a good bull called Foljambe
On the best two cows they could pick
One dropped a bull calf called Bolingbroke
The other a heifer they named, Phoenix.

These two half siblings they mated together
Producing a calf called Favorite from this mix
He in turn was put back to his mother
And sired a heifer called Young Phoenix.

Convinced they were on the right track
Of the type of cattle they wished to get
They mated Favorite to his half sister daughter
And produced the famous bull Comet.

They sold him for a 1,000 guineas
A price unheard of in 1810
But over the next 120 years
His worth was proved time and again.

For Comet was really the first sire
Of this stamp of beast to be born
So through the ingenuity of these two men
We have todays dual purpose Shorthorn.

Deep bodied, mossy coated cattle
That range from white, to red white and roan
Cows that can give up to a thousand gallons
And produce fleshy steers that are light of bone.

Shorthorns as improvers were reputed worldwide
But now a minority in the mists of time
Though reminders still appear on postcards and crockery
And numerous public house signs.

But sometimes at Ketton amongst the bought in cattle
Traces of Shorthorn still appear
And it takes me back to the 1950s
With memories I hold very dear.

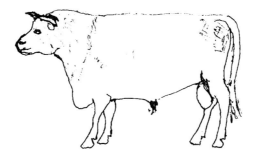

COMET

Another of Favourites' Famous Sons 1796-1807

The Durham Ox was a sensation
Weighing in at 216 stones
Carrying a massive amount of meat
On surprisingly small bones.

This unfortunately was his downfall
For one day he happened to slip
After being shown all over the country
He fell and dislocated his hip.

He was bred by Charles Colling of Ketton
And finally owned by a man called John Day
In five and a half years they toured three thousand miles
Drawn by horses in a converted dray.

Day wrote and published a pamphlet
Which he sold in every town they went through
He even had the beasts portrait painted
And sold two thousand prints of that too.

Two months after the accident
He had to have the beast slaughtered
It's dead weight was 189 stones
Before it was hung drawn and quartered.

Moss

Oh Moss my black and white trusty friend
I know on you I can depend
Working in dusty buildings on slats or straw
When moving sows, young pigs or boars
From pen to pen
Day in day out, and time again
While on the move you'll hear
My whistle clear
Or your brown eyes catch the movement of my hand
And in your own quiet way you take up the command
But now you're getting slow and your face is turning grey
And soon I fear will come the day
When your working life is through
But old lad, here's what we'll do
Come that time I'll take you home with me
And you can retire in comfort and luxury.

"Gemma" A Legend

I remember when I bought you
You were less than five months old
when along with your mother
To me you were sold.
You were so sweet and bambi like
And looked so small and fragile
Who would ever have thought
In time, we'd travel so many miles.
By two years old I had your yoked
And drove you out each day steady
At three we went on our first drive
Fourteen miles, for which you were quite ready
And proved that for a twelve hand pony
You had the stamina and power to stay
Everyone ended up talking about
Darlington Dave's little grey
At home we drove the country lanes
With club drives at weekends
Where ever we went you turned heads
And in three counties we made friends
But now alas, that's all past
Though folk still fondly speak your name
And reminisce about the little grey
That was always so smart and game.

The Burning Sensation

Oh dear, here comes the pain
Again, the one I dread and fear
I know what I must do
Head off in haste to the loo
For it gives very little warning, diarrhoea.

This complaint is most inconvenient
And unkind, Japanese flag comes to mind
Each morsel of food or drink of tea
Seems to go straight through me
It really is a bind.

I wish I could control this gastric bug
This thug, that's raging war inside my tum
I suppose I'll just have to wait and pray
That it does what the adverts say
And lets me get on with my day, this Immodium.

Waring Factions

I've Johnnie Walker in the cupboard
Arthritis in my joints and bones
And when one or the other is with me
I'm never alone
Sometimes they wrestle
When Johnnie tires Arthur causes pain
Then out comes Johnnie
And flattens Arthur again
I've seen doctors and specialists
But their tablets they can keep
For Johnnie Walker sees to it
That I get a good night's sleep.
There's only one downside
Causing a bit of panic
The lovely amber nectar
Is turning me into an alcoholic.

Geordie Pride

The Angel of the North stands proud
High upon a hill
Head in the clouds, feet on the ground
There to be viewed at will
For this great metal structure
Symbolises the people of Tyneside
Who stand erect with hearts of steel
And view their land with pride
For Geordie folk have every right
To be proud, even excited
About their buildings, bridges, art galleries
And Newcastle United
It's true the demise of ship building
And pit closures have left a gap
But the Metro Centre, and its guardian angel
Have put Tyneside back on the map.

Life and Death

What a fancy envelope
I wonder, what can it be?
Oh, it's a wedding invitation
Not my cup of tea.

She'll need a new rigout
Handbag, shoes, the lot
New hat and dress that
No one else has got.

That means endless hours of shopping
On which women seem to thrive
And by the time her wardrobe she's acquired
I'll feel more dead than alive.

She'll work up to a fever
As we approach this appointed date
It'll be don't do this and don't that
You're going to make us late.

Then there's all the expense and protocol
Promises made by the bride and groom
And when the honeymoon period's over
Life could be all doom and gloom.

For a tuppeny bun now costs fourpence
And he's no longer his own master
Worse still if they split and there's children
It's a recipe for disaster.

Oh, give me a good funeral
The facts are there, much better by far
You're celebrating a past life
And you know just where you are.

Oh Yes there's a sadness
But life has to carry on
You just have to remember them for what they were
And accept they're dead and gone.

For the deceased have a history
They've competed in life's race
One can speak of their achievements
And know they've gone to a better place.

For whether they're cremated
Or laid beneath the sod
We believe as Christians
They're in the care of God.

Unfortunate

Now I'm going to tell you a story
Which believe it or not is said to be true
It was told to me by a friend
And relates to a couple she once knew.

It's about a house-proud woman
And her husband, poor hen pecked bloke
For the wife is no uncertain terms insisted
That outdoors was the place if he wanted to smoke.

But one day it was raining stair rods
And she was out shopping and he fancied a fag
He thought while sitting on the loo
That he'd have a crafty drag.

Now the wife had just cleaned the bathroom
And with detergent given the bowl a spray
But he never gave it a thought
As he sat blissfully puffing away.

Till he heard the front door opening
Then thought, hell, I'll be a dead man
So without the slightest hesitation
Dropped his half smoked cigarette down the pan.

He rose with the immediate explosion
Crying out like some demented creature
As a red hot burning sensation
Attacked one might say his best feature.

His wife on hearing the commotion
Shot upstairs in a hell of a hurry
To be greeted by her husband dancing about
His face sick with pain and worry.

She soaked a towel in cold water
And said till the ambulance comes this will do fine
Now stand still and keep it pressed on
While I go down and ring 999.

The ambulance seemed to take ages to arrive
When told the men had big grins on their faces
In fact they laughed so much that they dropped him
And broke his leg in two places.

So now he's hospitalised and immobile
And his visitors come in laughing and joking
But he doesn't think it funny at all
And he's definitely given up smoking.

A Stinging Conversation

When visiting a strange town one day
I stopped the motor and asked the way
To where access I wished to gain
A place called Honey Pot Lane
The lady said "Could you have got it wrong
Are you sure it's not just slang
We have Wasps Nest Avenue
That's where all the cranky old women moved to
And then there's Bees Knees Drive
Where all the posh poverty stricken survive
Or directions to Clover Hill I can give
Where all the honest hard workers live
But it really is quite absurd
Of Honey Pot Lane I've never heard".

Wishes

Oh How I wish some instrument I could play
And spend my time
Each hour of each day.

In some temperate climb
Making love, music and poetry
Creating rhythm, scan and rhyme.

I feel potential deep in me
Wanting to surface, to be uncovered
And burst out free.

Yet if my talent was discovered
And I sprung to sudden fame
Would I be bothered?

All I wish at the end of the day
Is to be remembered for what I've had to say.

The Poor Beggar Didn't Stand a Chance

We'd just finished our dinner
And at the dining table were still all sat round
When from somewhere in the lounge
There came a buzzing sound.

My wife jumped to attention
Alerted by the noise
Armed herself with aerosol and swatter
Determined to find the owner of the voice.

Now this black and yellow intruder
Was at the window and only trying to get out
When she squirted it then with the swatter
Gave it one almighty clout.

But she only managed to stun it
And knock it to the floor
And being quite intelligent the poor creature
Decided to keep schtum and leg it for the door.

Now my wife as if on a big game hunt
Had murder in her eyes
For she has a deep hatred
Of beetles, wasps and flies.

And so with fear and determination
Written all over her face
She squirted and battered the poor creature
Till there was bits of it scattered all over the place.

I'd watched in disbelief
Thinking I'm glad that wasn't me
As with a look of exhausted satisfaction
She sat down to drink her tea.

Ah, Sure, It Could Only Happen In Ireland

I was walking down Dublin's main street one day
When into a pub I made my way
Piano music filled the air
But I couldn't see one anywhere
But a group of men were gathered round
From whence came the sound
After buying my pint I made my way
And thought, Lord is this my first drink today?

For a little elf in a really professional manner
Was playing a tune on a tiny grand piano
And above the gabble of rich Irish brogues
A bunch of loveable rogues
Sang heartily along
The words to some familiar song.

The barman, my thoughts must have read
Because he said
"He's good for business that's quite plain
He certainly knows how to entertain
Keeping the party atmosphere going
And the Guinness flowing"
"How did you come by the little chap?
What good fortune", "yes but really a mishap"
"Please tell", "okay, I can't pretend
That it's a secret my friend."

"You see the man in the corner over there
With the ice-blue eyes, beard, and long white hair
If you were to buy him a Guinness and a whisky or two
I'm sure he'd grant a wish for you"
So over to the corner I made my way
The beverages all on a tray.
I looked at him, he said "Pull up a chair"
He rubbed his hands then stroked his facial hair

I said "To judge now I'm in no position
But I've heard that you're a magician"
So I did
"And I'm desperately in need of a few quid"
"Ah, well, buy another round for me
Then just wait a day or two and see
And I'll do what I can
So I will, my man".

So a week later I happened to be
Once again in that vicinity
So I popped in to the very same pub
For a pint and a bite of grub
The barman said "How did it go mate?"
I said "Listen here, and I'll bring you up to date".

"The days passed and nothing came
I thought my investment had been in vain
Then on the third day, Oh an awful smell,
From where it came I couldn't tell
Then the neighbours started to complain
Next the council workmen came
Dug up the garden, and tore the house apart
They all but broke my heart
So they did for sure
They ripped out cupboards and the boards up from the floor".

"They found the cause, so they did
Thousands and thousands of rotting squid"
Sipping his Guinness and scratching his head
The barman finally said
"I know it isn't funny
But I'll be thinking you asked for money?"

And then with baited breath
Added, "Did I not mention he was a little deaf?
How do you think it came to be
That I have a Leprechaun like he
Do you think at the time
I'd partaken of so much black slime
That I was so Brahms and Liste
I'd asked for a ten inch pianist?"

When I am Old

When I am old I shall wear outrageous clothes
And not give a damn about fashion
I shall be in whatever mood I like
And follow each of my whims with passion.

When I am old I shall do as I like
Go where and whenever I please
Say what I think and sod everyone else
Just live life as free as the breeze.

When I am old I shall eat when I want
And do just for me what feels right
Perhaps lying in bed half of each day
And staying out late every night.

When I am old I might be in pain
My old bones may creak and groan
Be hard of hearing, have bad eyesight
Now that would give me reason to moan.

When I am old, just hang on a minute
All this seems familiar somehow
Who needs to be old to be like that
For it's just the way I am now.

Hope

We are but tenants in this life
For things are only loaned to us
No matter how much they've cost to acquire
We must leave them behind without any fuss.

For we come into this world with nothing
And take nothing with us, when we leave
Except to hope that we've done to others
That which we would have liked to receive.

So when we shuffle off our mortal coil
And leave our hard won chattels behind
All we can do is hope others will appreciate
And in them the same pleasure as us find.

And so in some small way when we are gone
Hope to have left something that can be carried on.